# nickelodeon™

# 5-Minute Stories Collection

Random House 🏠 New York

# CONTENTS

# ICE TEAM

It was a sunny day, and the PAW Patrol was getting ready for a big trip to see their friend Jake at the ice fields. Suddenly, there was a loud roar and a giant truck rolled up.

"That's a totally awesome truck!" Zuma barked.

"Is this how we're going on our road trips now?" Chase asked.

"Yes," Ryder replied. "Presenting the PAW Patroller! It's a Lookout on wheels. It can take us anywhere!"

Ryder pressed a button on his PupPad. A door in the side of the Patroller yawned open and a mechanical dog hopped out.

"Robo Dog will be our driver!"

Inside the PAW Patroller was a hangout room, a snack machine, and space for all of the team's vehicles. As Ryder was showing the pups around the truck, their friend Jake called on the PupPad.

"Hey, Jake! How are the ice fields?" Ryder asked.

"Amazing!" Jake declared. "Take a look!" The screen showed snowy hills and an icy river. "Bring lots of treats. You get seriously hungry out here. Speaking of which, it's time for a granola bar."

Jake set down his pack, placed the phone in a side pocket, and dug out a snack. Suddenly, he slipped on the ice, and the pups could hear him shout, "My phone! My maps! All my stuff!"

Jake's pack slid down a snowy hill. He chased after it.

"Be careful, Jake!" Ryder cautioned.

"I've got it! I've got it!" Jake yelled as he jumped to grab the bag. "Oh, no! I don't have it!"

The pack with all of Jake's equipment fell into an icy river. The screen in the PAW Patroller went black.

"Jake's in big trouble!" Rubble exclaimed.

"Pups, get your vehicles," Ryder said. "It's time for a road trip!"

The PAW Patroller's back door opened and a ramp came out. The pups quickly drove their vehicles aboard. Robo Dog started the engine, and the PAW Patroller rolled into action.

At the ice fields, Jake tried to get his backpack out of the water. But the riverbank was so icy that he began to slide in! Luckily, a husky pup pulled him back out.

"Sweet save!" Jake said, then introduced himself.

"My name's Everest!" the pup exclaimed. "I rescued someone! I've always wanted to do a real rescue."

"We should probably get going," Everest said. "A storm's rolling in. I wouldn't want to lose my first real rescue in a blizzard. We can wait it out in my igloo. To get there, we can do this. . . ."

Everest flopped onto her belly and slid
down the hill.

"Belly-bogganing!" Jake shouted, taking
off after her. "Look out below!"

The two new friends slid along on the ice,
zooming past some penguins.

When the PAW Patroller reached the ice fields, the snow was falling hard. The team started to look for Jake. They quickly found his frozen phone and pack.

"This means Jake doesn't have any supplies," Ryder said. Then he noticed something in the snow. "Are those tracks?"

Chase gave the tracks a sniff. "That's Jake,
all right! And he's got another pup with him."
"Those tracks should lead us to Jake,"
Ryder announced. "Let's follow them."

As Chase followed the tracks on the ground, Skye took to the frosty air. "This pup's got to fly!" she said.

"Any sign of Jake?" Ryder asked over the radio.

"No," she replied. "Just snow, snow, and more snow." But then, off in the distance, Skye thought she saw something.

Everest and Jake came to a narrow bridge that stretched across a deep, dark ravine. "My igloo is just across that ice bridge," Everest said.

"Will it hold us?" Jake asked.

"I hope so," the husky replied. "It's the only way to get over."

As they walked across, they heard a terrible noise: *Crinkle! Crackle!* The ice bridge was breaking!

Just as the bridge collapsed, Skye swooped in, catching Jake and Everest with a cable. But before she had carried them to the other side of the ravine, the rope broke.

"Jump!" Jake yelled.

Everest landed on a ledge, but Jake missed it.
He caught the edge with his fingers and dangled
over the dark ravine.

"Don't worry!" Everest called. "I've got you!"
She snagged Jake's sleeve and pulled him to safety.
"Yes—two rescues in one day!"

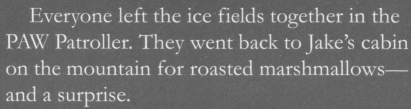

Everyone left the ice fields together in the PAW Patroller. They went back to Jake's cabin on the mountain for roasted marshmallows— and a surprise.

"Everest," Jake said, "I could use a smart pup like you to help out on the mountain."

"And for saving Jake and showing great rescue skills," Ryder added, "I'd like to make you an official member of the PAW Patrol!"

"This is the best day ever!" Everest exclaimed, and all the pups cheered.

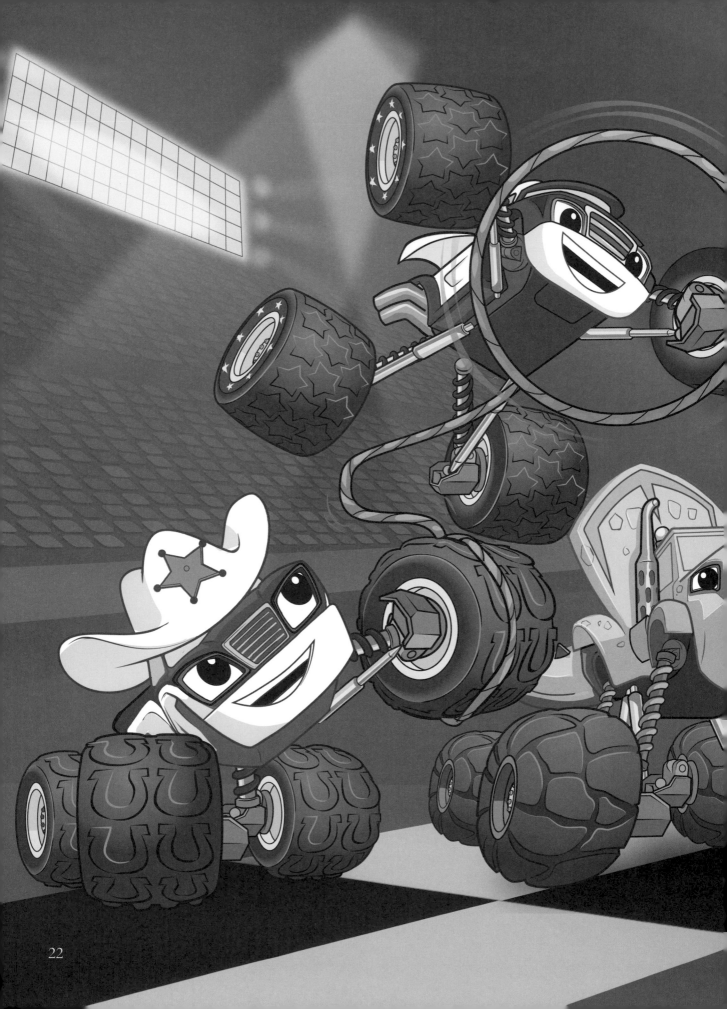

It was the day of the Monster Machine World Championship race, and Blaze and his friends were excited to compete! Stripes the tiger truck growled, Starla the cowgirl truck twirled her lasso, and Darington the stunt truck practiced amazing jumps. Zeg the dinosaur truck roared happily.

"This is gonna be great!" exclaimed AJ, Blaze's driver and best friend.

But before the race could start, a cheating
Monster Machine named Crusher used
Trouble Bubbles to carry all the racers away!

Blaze and AJ landed in the middle of a desert. As they raced back to the track, they saw Stripes dangling from a cliff. He was tangled in some vines that were starting to break!

Blaze spotted a pair of rocks shaped like ramps. "If we drive really fast," he said, "we can use one of those rocks to jump to Stripes!"

AJ switched on his Visor View to figure
out which ramp would reach Stripes.

Then Blaze zoomed up to rescue his
friend. He reached the tiger truck just as
the last vine snapped. Stripes was saved!

Blaze and Stripes continued to make their way back to the racetrack. They entered a forest and saw Darington being chased by a pack of Grizzly Trucks! "Run!" cried Darington.

The Monster Machines reached a river, where
they found a curved piece of wood.
"The curved wood has tall sides to keep the
water out!" said Blaze, and he launched it into
the water. The Monster Machines jumped on
and floated to safety.

Back on land, the Monster Machines spotted Zeg tumbling down a mountain. Blaze caught the dinosaur truck with his tow hook.

Then the machines found Starla at the bottom of a hole inside a cave. Working together, they used a pulley to haul her out. "Now let's hurry and get back to the race!" Blaze said.

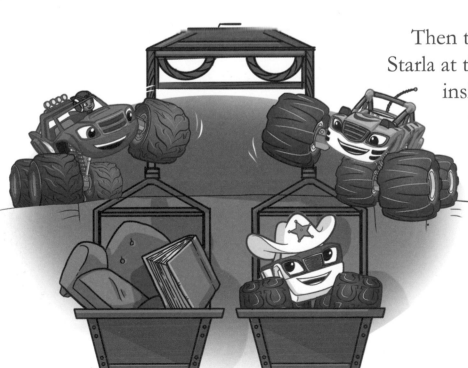

The Monster Machines arrived at the track just in time for the start of the competition.

"This race is mine, Blaze," growled Crusher. "No one is gonna beat me."

Blaze smiled. "We'll just see about that."

"On your marks, get set, GO!" cried the announcer.

While Blaze and his friends had fun soaring across ramps and twisting through loops with one another, Crusher could only think of one thing—winning.

"A little cheating ought to slow those guys down!" Crusher said, cackling. He swerved left and right, knocking oil barrels, hay bales, and stacked tires onto the track.

"Look out!" called Stripes.

*"Whoooaaa!"* cried Starla.

Darington slipped in some oil and spun out.

Zeg's tires got trapped in the hay bales.

But one Monster Machine hurtled
through the mess, leaping high over
the puddles of oil and dodging the
tires and hay bales. It was Blaze!
  "Come on, Blaze!" cheered the
other Monster Machines.

AJ looked ahead. "Crusher is almost at the finish line!"

"We need to use Blazing Speed!" Blaze deployed his spoiler and boosters. *"Let's blaaaze!"*

Blaze hit a ramp and did a huge flip in the air. He landed and zoomed forward—just ahead of Crusher!

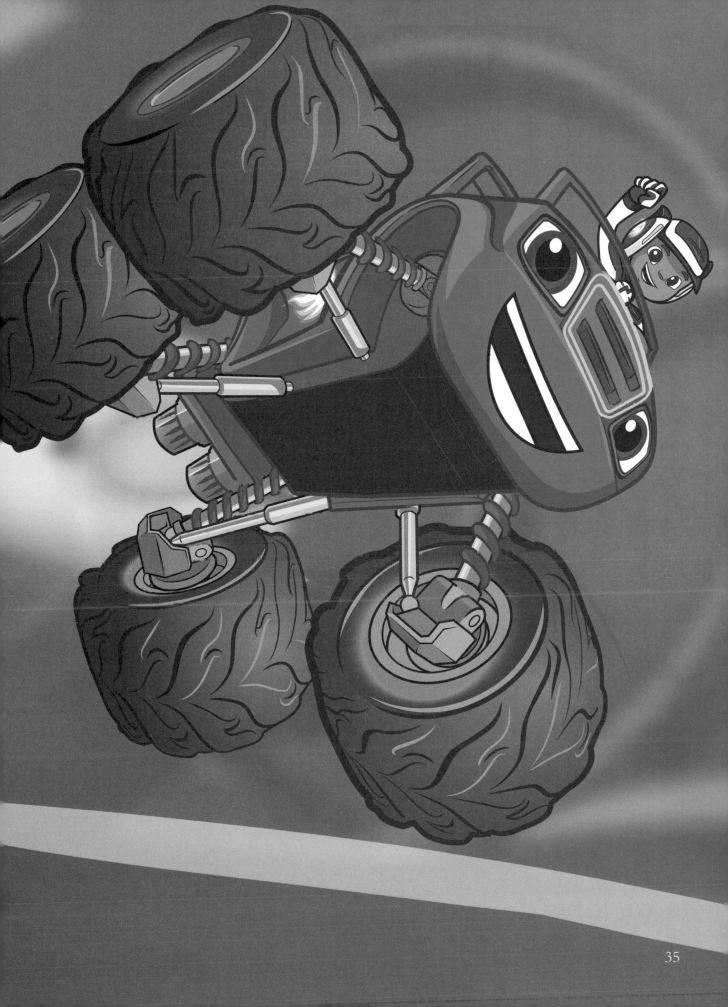

"Blaze! You just won the Monster Machine World Championship. What are you going to do next?" asked the announcer.

"Well . . . I think I'd like to hang out with my friends." Blaze grinned at them. "You wanna go around the track again?"

"*Woo-hoo!*" the Monster Machines cheered.

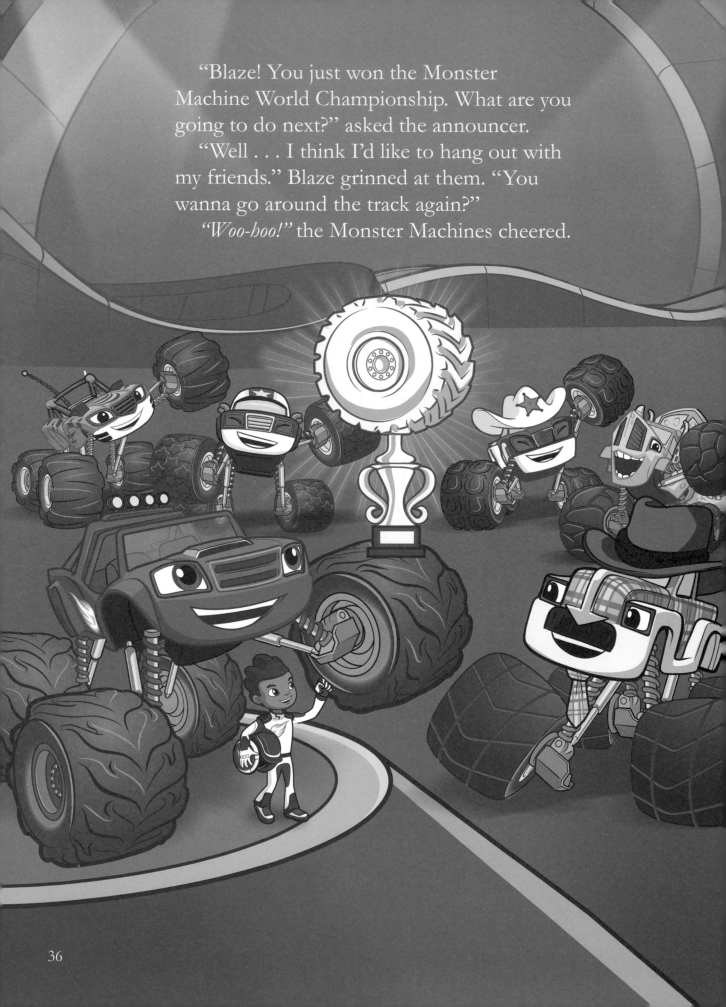

# THE PUPS SAVE THE BUNNIES

It was a sunny day, and Mr. Porter was visiting
Farmer Yumi to get some carrots for his market.
But there was a problem . . . the carrots were
disappearing into the dirt!

Farmer Yumi knew exactly what was really
happening—bunnies were eating her carrots.

This was a job for the PAW Patrol!

Ryder called the PAW Patrol to the Lookout and told them about the bunnies.

"We need to move the bunnies to a field where they'll be safe and won't eat Farmer Yumi's carrots. Rubble, I'll need your shovel so we can find the bunnies' tunnels."

"Rubble on the double!" he yelped.
"And, Chase, I'll need your
megaphone and herding skills to round
up the bunnies," Ryder continued.
"Chase is on the case!" the police
pup exclaimed.

41

Ryder, Rubble, and Chase raced to Farmer Yumi's farm. "Let's dig in!" Rubble said, and he started digging for the bunny tunnels. "I think I found something!" he shouted a few moments later. "In fact, I found *two* somethings!"

Ryder needed a way to carry the two bunnies from the farm. He called Rocky and Skye on his PupPad. "Rocky, can you get some old kennel cages so Skye can fly them here?"

"Don't lose it—reuse it!" Rocky said.

"And I'll be there in two shakes of a bunny's tail," Skye added.

Skye arrived with the kennel cages, and Chase started herding the bunnies into them.

"Attention, all bunnies!" Chase announced
through his megaphone. "We've brought
cages with nice, soft beds to take you to your
new homes."

"And inside each cage," Skye said, "is a
crunchy treat."

The bunnies hopped into the cages, and
Skye lifted off in her copter to take them to
their new field.

But the busy day wasn't over yet! When Mr. Porter returned to his market, he found some furry-tailed surprises in the box of vegetables he'd brought from the farm.

This was another job for the PAW Patrol!

The team sped to Mr. Porter's market. The bunnies were everywhere. They were burrowing under the apples and bouncing on the bananas.

"I need some of your delicious carrot cake, Mr. Porter," Ryder said. He had a plan for how to collect the bunnies.

Ryder set the cake on the ground, and all the bunnies bounded over to it. "Now we need your net, Chase!"

Chase launched his net over the bunnies, and Ryder carefully scooped them up.

Skye carried the last of the bunnies to their new home in the faraway field. It was the perfect place for them—they couldn't bother anyone, and no one would bother them. As soon as Ryder opened the kennel cages, the little bunnies bounced into the grass and began to happily munch on flowers.

"Bye-bye, bunnies," Skye said. "I'm going to miss you . . . and you . . . and you . . . and you."

"I think they're going to be pretty happy out here," Ryder declared.

When Skye returned to the Lookout, she realized she wasn't alone—a bunny had stowed away with her!

"Can we keep her?" she asked.

"We can handle one bunny," Ryder said.

"Ryder, you're the best," Skye cheered as the pups welcomed their new furry friend.

# A Tale of Two Genies

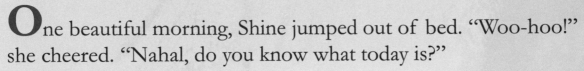

One beautiful morning, Shine jumped out of bed. "Woo-hoo!" she cheered. "Nahal, do you know what today is?"

Nahal yawned.

"It's the day that Shimmer and I become genies!" Shine explained.

The sleepy tiger crawled back under the covers.

"Come on!" Shine insisted. "Let's go wake up Shimmer!"

But Shimmer wasn't in her
bed. She wasn't under her
vanity table. She wasn't in her
wardrobe closet.

"Where in the genie world
did she go?" Shine asked.
"Come on, Nahal. Let's look
downstairs!"

In the living room, Shine spotted a collection of pretty genie bottles. Suddenly, one began to shake. Out popped Shimmer and Tala!

"What's with all the bottles?" Shine asked.

"I'm looking for the perfect one to give to our new friend!" Shimmer explained.

Shine laughed. "We can't use just any old genie bottle! We have to make a new one!"

The two sisters gathered super-special ingredients, and, using their magic, they made a new, beautiful bottle!

It was perfect. But who would they give it to?

The twins ran to ask the Magic Mirror. The mirror
showed them the perfect friend for them—someone
patient, fun, kindhearted, brave, and unique!

The genies used the Magic Mirror to send the genie
bottle into the human world. It attached itself to a
necklace in a carnival booth!

At the carnival booth, a girl named Leah knocked over some milk bottles with a ball. "We have a winner!" the man at the booth announced. "And what would the lucky winner like for a prize?"

Leah wanted the necklace. But her best friend, Zac, said, "Ooh! Get the walkie-talkies!" Giggling, Leah agreed.

The man in charge of the game
was impressed that Leah had chosen
a prize for her friend. So he let her
pick out another prize. Leah chose
the pretty necklace.

Leah went over to the fun house. She laughed at her reflection in the funny mirrors.

She noticed that the bottle on her new necklace was glowing. Curious, she rubbed the bottle. Colorful smoke and sparkles swirled out of it!

"What's happening?" she asked.

*Poof!* Leah couldn't believe her eyes! Two girls, a little monkey, and a baby tiger were standing before her. Shimmer and Shine hugged Leah tightly.

"It's so nice to finally meet you!" Shine bubbled.

"Yeah, you too," said Leah, confused. "Who are you?"

"I'm Shimmer!" said the girl with the shiny pink ponytail.
"I'm Shine," said the one with the big lavender eyes.
Together they chimed, "Your genies divine!"
"We're here to grant you three wishes a day!" Shine explained.
"There's no way you're real genies," Leah said.

Using their genie magic, Shimmer and Shine
made skateboards, sundaes, and a tree house
appear out of thin air!

"Now do you believe us?" Shine asked.

Leah was amazed. "Yes!" she cried.

Leah laughed and hugged the genies. "I'm so lucky to have my very own genies!"

Shimmer said, "You're patient, fun, kindhearted, brave, and unique."

Shine added, "So *we're* the lucky ones to have *you*!"

# DRIVING FORCE!

E ngines roared and fans cheered—the big race at the Monster Dome was on! As Blaze turned the last corner, Crusher was the only one ahead of him.

"Give me some speed," Blaze said to his driver and best buddy, AJ. Blaze shot forward with a burst of Blazing Speed, zooming past Crusher and across the finish line!

"We won!" Blaze and AJ cheered.

One morning, Starla wasn't feeling well. Gabby the mechanic checked her engine.

"You're missing one of your pistons!" Gabby said. "They pull gas and air into your engine. Then there's a spark, and—BOOM!—the engine makes power so you can drive!"

"We need to find Starla's piston," AJ said.
"Switching to Visor View."

He turned on his special visor to search
for the missing piston. "There it is!" he
announced. "Starla's piston is in that swamp!"

Crusher overheard and whispered to Pickle,
"If I get that piston, it'll give my engine extra
power! I'll be the best Monster Machine
in the whole world!"

"I don't think that's how it
works," Pickle said as he
raced after Crusher.

Crusher and Pickle raced away from Axle City in search of the piston. Blaze and AJ were just behind them the entire way. As Crusher entered the swamp, he knew he had to stop Blaze from getting to the piston first. He got an idea. He would make a giant pineapple blaster!

Blaze and AJ were zooming toward
the swamp when . . . *Splat! Splat! Splat!*
Pineapples crashed down around Blaze.

"Gaskets!" he exclaimed. "Those
pineapples are everywhere!"

Blaze thought for a moment.
"We need to knock them away using
something with a lot of force—like a
crane with a big, heavy wrecking ball!"

"First we need outriggers so the crane won't tip over," Blaze continued. "And to swing the wrecking ball, we need a hydraulic boom with a steel cable. Last but not least, we need our wrecking ball."

Blaze and AJ quickly made the parts to turn Blaze into a wrecking crane Monster Machine! Blaze swung the big ball and knocked away each pineapple, one by one.

The last pineapple hit Crusher's pineapple blaster and broke it!

"Nice shot!" AJ cheered.

"Now let's hurry and get that piston before Crusher does!" AJ said.

"Give me some speed!" Blaze exclaimed, and they rocketed off through the woods.

Meanwhile, Pickle spotted the piston in a mud pit.
"That's it!" Crusher exclaimed. "I finally found it!"
"Technically, *I* found it," Pickle pointed out.
But Crusher didn't hear him. The big truck swung
his tow cable and hooked the piston. "Now I'll be the
best Monster Machine in the whole world!"

But as Crusher started to pull the piston out of the mud, another cable grabbed on to it.

"It's Blaze!" Pickle cheered.

Blaze tugged on the piston. "That belongs to Starla, not you!" he said.

Crusher's engine roared as he tugged back. "It's mine now!"

Blaze's and Crusher's engines thundered. Their tires kicked up dirt. The two trucks pulled back and forth. Finally, Blaze pulled with so much force that he tugged Crusher into the mud pit! The piston flew into the air and AJ caught it!

Blaze and AJ raced back to the Monsterdome to give the piston to Starla. Gabby put it in Starla's engine.

The cowgirl truck revved her engine. "Yee-haw! I'm fixed!"

All the Monster Machines cheered, and AJ gave Blaze a high tire! To celebrate, the trucks sped off for a race, with Blaze and Starla leading the way!

# LET'S SAVE PIRATE DAY!

It was the day of the big pirate festival in Playa Verde, the city where Dora lived. Dora's mami had organized the festival to raise money to turn the city's old fort into a museum.

"I can't wait for the pirate ship to get here!" Dora said. "I'm going to take everyone out to sea!"

But then Mami came over looking sad.
"The pirate ship isn't coming today," she said.
"Oh, no!" said Kate. "We need the pirate
ship to make enough money for the museum!"

"But how do we take a pirate ship ride if
there's no pirate ship?" asked Pablo.

Dora saw a rowboat at the dock. "I have a
great idea!" she told her friends. "Maybe we can
build our own pirate ship with some stuff from
the museum basement. *¡Vámonos, amigos!*"

When Dora and her friends got to the basement, they found sails and a flag in no time.

"All we need now is a wheel," said Kate.

"Here it is!" Pablo cried. But when he started to pull on the wheel, it pulled him!

"That wheel must be enchanted!" said Dora. "Cool!"

Dora jumped up and grabbed the wheel.
"Come find us, Kate!" she called over her
shoulder as she and Pablo flew off.

The magic wheel carried Dora and Pablo to a hidden cave, where they found an enchanted pirate ship. When the pirate ship saw Dora, it said, "*¡La Capitán Malencua has regresado!* You've returned!"

Dora was surprised. "I'm not your pirate captain," she said.

"Ah, you look just like her," the pirate ship told Dora.

"Who's *la Capitán Malencua*?" asked Pablo.

"She was a good and kind pirate," the pirate ship explained. "When bad pirates stole treasure from the people, *la Capitán Malencua* used her magic charm bracelet to stop them and return the treasure!"

"Long ago, *la Capitán Malencua* asked me to protect some of the treasure," continued the pirate ship. "She put the treasure on board and hid me in this cave. To unlock the treasure, you must turn the wheel in your hands."

Dora and Pablo turned the wheel, and a treasure chest rose from the ship!

Suddenly, a band of mean-looking pirates swung onto the deck.

"You found it!" the pirate captain crowed. "My great-great-grandfather tried to get this treasure. Now, finally, it's mine, mine, mine!"

The pirates grabbed the treasure and sped away in their ship.

"We've got to get the treasure back!" Dora exclaimed.

The ship showed Dora the magic charm bracelet on the wheel. "*La Capitán Malencua* said whoever tried to help me should have her magic bracelet."

Dora put on the bracelet. "We need to scare those bad pirates so we can get the treasure back. Which charm can we use?"

"Definitely the dragon!" Dora and Pablo said together.

"To get the dragon to appear, we need to say '*¡Dragón mágico!*'" Dora said.

As soon as they spoke the magic words,
a dragon flew out of the charm! He hissed
fiercely at the pirates, scooped up the chest,
and took the treasure back to the ship.
"Now let's get out of here!" cried Dora.

The enchanted ship floated through the
cave. But the mean pirates were right behind
them, firing their cannons!

"We've got to go faster," said Kate. "We
need more wind!"

Suddenly, Pablo sneezed. *"Ahhh-chooo!"*

"Hey! *Tengo una idea*," said Dora. "If we can get *el dragon* to sneeze, he can blow the ship out of the cave."

Pablo threw some peppery popcorn into the dragon's mouth. The dragon gobbled the snack and sneezed a big, loud *"Ahhhhhh-choooo!"* The sneeze filled the sails with wind!

The magic pirate ship sailed out of the cave,
leaving the mean pirates behind.

"Thank you for saving the treasure!" the
pirate ship told Dora and her friends as they
headed back to the festival.

To let people know they were on their way with the pirate ship, Dora and her friends shouted "Yo ho ho!" as loud as they could.

Dora looked through the telescope. "They heard us!" she cheered. "They're coming back!"

Everyone was excited to play on the pirate ship!
Dora's *mami* was proud of Dora and her
friends. "Now we will have enough money to
open the museum. Thank you for saving the day!"
"You *arrrr* welcome!" Dora said in her best
pirate voice.

# RUBBLE TO THE RESCUE!

One morning at the Lookout, Rubble bounded into the living room. *Apollo the Super Pup* was on. It was his favorite television show!

Rubble watched, fascinated, as Apollo pulled off another daring rescue.

"I want to save the day my own way!" Rubble said.

When the other pups went to play soccer with Ryder, Rubble decided to play Super Pup. "Hmm, who can I save?" he wondered aloud.

Rubble passed by City Hall, where he ran into Mayor Goodway.

"Rubble!" she said. "The train engineer called to say there's been a rockslide!"

"The train is stuck inside Mountain Tunnel,"
Mayor Goodway continued. "Can you get
Ryder and the PAW Patrol to help?"

"Don't worry, Mayor Goodway." Rubble
raced to the rockslide.

But he didn't alert Ryder and the other pups!

"Where is the PAW Patrol?" the train engineer asked Rubble when he arrived.

"We don't need Ryder and the PAW Patrol." Rubble struck a hero pose. "Rubble the Super Pup can handle this, just like Apollo the Super Pup does—on my own!"

Rubble started to push the boulders off the
train tracks.

"Looks like more boulders could come down if
we're not careful," said the train engineer.

"Stand back. I'll take care of this in no time!"
As Rubble heaved the last boulder out of the way,
sure enough, some rocks came tumbling down!

Rubble and the train engineer scrambled to get out of the way.

"Oops," said Rubble. He had caused another rockslide. Now he and the train engineer were trapped inside Mountain Tunnel!

Rubble hung his head. "I'm sorry. I didn't save the day. I just made everything worse."

"That's okay, Rubble," said the train engineer. "You were just trying to help. But what should we do now?"

"Call Ryder and the PAW Patrol!" barked Rubble.

Ryder called the PAW Patrol together when he heard that Rubble was in trouble.

"Chase," he said, "I need your winch to move the rocks out of the way. And Zuma, I need you to drive Rubble's rig. We need his truck to remove the rest of the rocks once we get him out."

"The PAW Patrol is on the roll!" the pups shouted.

When they reached Mountain Tunnel, Chase threw a winch around a rock. He pulled it off the slide, leaving a small hole. "Rubble, can you squeeze through?" he called.

Wriggling with all his might, Rubble broke free of the rockslide!

"Okay, Rubble, you know what to do," said Ryder.

Rubble climbed aboard his digger. "Rubble on the double!" he called.

The hardworking pup scooped up boulder after boulder and pushed them off the tracks. In no time, he had cleared the tunnel!

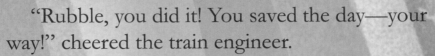

"Rubble, you did it! You saved the day—your way!" cheered the train engineer.

Rubble shook his head. "You mean I *helped* save the day."

The engineer nodded. "You're right. Thanks, Ryder—and you pups, too!"

Ryder waved goodbye as the train chugged out of the tunnel. "You're welcome. And whenever you're in trouble, just yelp for help!"

Ryder and the pups took the rest of the afternoon off to play in the backyard.

"Let's all play together—the PAW Patrol way," barked Rubble.

"Agreed," giggled Chase and Zuma.

# The Sweetest Cupcake

Leah and her best friend, Zac, had spent the morning trying to make cupcakes. But all they had made was a big mess!

Leah frowned. "I promised to bring cupcakes to the school bake sale tomorrow, but I can't make a single one!"

Zac's belly grumbled. "I'm heading home for a pre-cupcake snack," he said.

"A wish! That's it!" she said. "I'll ask my genies-in-training for help!" She rubbed the bottle on her necklace.

*"Shimmer and Shine, my genies divine, through this special chant, three wishes you'll grant!"* And with that, the genies appeared in Leah's kitchen!

"What's cookin', Leah?" asked Shine, tossing her blue hair.

"Nothing," Leah admitted. "But I need to wish for a cupcake!"

Shimmer said the magic words: *"Boom, Zahramay! First wish of the day!"*

*Poof!* A giant cake teetering on a tiny teacup appeared!

125

Leah giggled. "That's a cup of cake, not a cupcake." She checked a recipe card. "To make a real cupcake, we need to mix a few ingredients together."

But Leah was out of ingredients. So for her second wish, she wished for eggs, milk, and flour.

*"Boom, Zahramay! Second wish of the day!"* Shimmer chanted.

The genies conjured up a chicken for eggs, a cow for milk, and a basket of . . . *flowers?*

"Only the freshest ingredients!" Shimmer said proudly.

But the only one who liked eating flowers was the cow!

"I was just hoping for a carton of eggs, a gallon of milk, and a bag of flour," said Leah.

Shimmer frowned. "Oh, sprinkles. I didn't get this wish right, either!"

A voice called out, "Hey, Leah! You still in there?" It was Zac—and he was coming into the kitchen!

"Hurry!" Leah cried to the genies. "Help me move the cow into the other room!" They tried pushing the cow out of the kitchen, but she wouldn't budge. Since the cow liked to eat flowers, Shine used them to lead her into the living room.

"The wrong kind of flower is turning out to be just the right kind!" Shine laughed.

Leah and the genies tried to milk the cow and get the chicken to lay eggs, but it was taking a long time.

"I wish we could speed this up!" Leah said.

Shimmer twirled her bracelets. *"Boom, Zahramay! Third wish of the day!"*

Suddenly, a rumbling conveyer belt
appeared. Buckets were filled with milk,
and the chicken started laying eggs.
Everyone worked as fast as they could.
"Guys, I don't think I can keep up!"
Leah shouted.

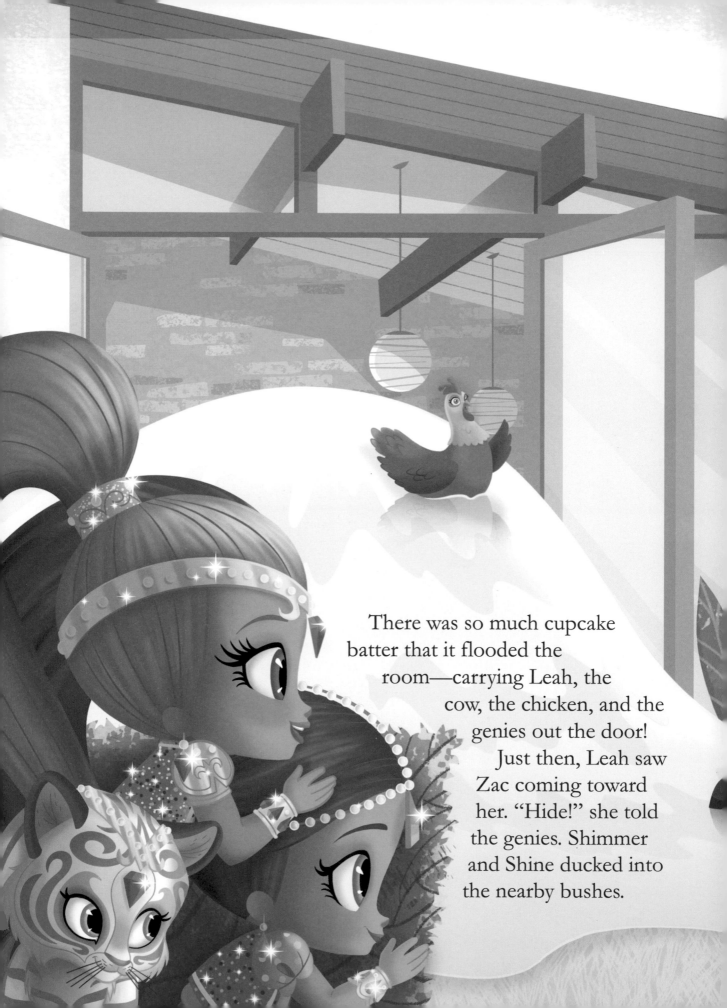

There was so much cupcake batter that it flooded the room—carrying Leah, the cow, the chicken, and the genies out the door! Just then, Leah saw Zac coming toward her. "Hide!" she told the genies. Shimmer and Shine ducked into the nearby bushes.

But Zac had already noticed the cow and the chicken. "You use fresh ingredients," he said. "No wonder your cake tastes great!"

Zac showed Leah the cupful of cake he was
holding. He'd scooped it from the giant cake
Shimmer had conjured. "I couldn't find a plate,
so I'm taking this cup of cake home with me."
Then he walked back to his house.

"A cup!" Leah smiled. "Shimmer! Shine!
I know what to do now!"

Back in the kitchen, Leah took a mug and scooped a cupful of cake. She turned the mug over—and out popped a mini cake!

"You made a cupcake from a cup of cake!" said Shimmer. "Great idea!"

Leah and the genies scooped, frosted, and decorated enough cupcakes for the bake sale.

"Who knew all our mistakes could make such a sweet little dessert?" laughed Shimmer.

Leah agreed. "Another mistake turned out great!"

# THE PUPPY AND THE RING

Long ago in the land of Bubbledom, there lived a Sun King. Every morning, he made the sun rise with the power of his magic ring—the Ring of the Sun.

Everyone agreed that having both day and
night was a wonderful thing—everyone but
the Night Wizard. He wanted it to be night
forever. So he sent his lobster army to the
Sun King's realm to steal the Ring of the Sun.

The Night Wizard's army marched
through Bubbledom to the Sun King's castle.
They charged into the throne room and
zapped the Sun King and his guards with
magic sleeping moonbeams!

After the Sun King fell asleep, the army
took the ring and hid it in a treasure chest.
Then they started their long journey back
to the Night Wizard's realm.

As they marched through Bubbledom, the
Night Wizard's lobster army came upon Gil
and Molly. The Guppies were selling delicious
lemon Bubble Slushies. It was a hot day, and
the lobster soldiers were very thirsty. Soon
everyone was in line to get a cool drink.

While the lobster soldiers were drinking
their slushies, Bubble Puppy bumped into
the treasure chest. The lid opened, revealing
the Ring of the Sun. When Bubble Puppy
went to take a closer look, the ring attached
itself around his neck!

"Seize the puppy! Seize them all!" cried the lobster general when he saw the ring on Bubble Puppy.

"Run!" shouted Gil. He, Molly, and Bubble Puppy dashed into the forest. The lobster army followed close behind.

Gil, Molly, and Bubble Puppy raced into the woods. Suddenly, the magical Flutterguppies, Deema and Oona, appeared! They gasped when they saw the Ring of the Sun around Bubble Puppy's neck.

"If the Sun King doesn't have the ring when the sun goes down tonight, the sun will never come up again!" said Oona. The two Flutterguppies decided to take Gil, Molly, and Bubble Puppy to the Sun King's castle to return the ring.

On the way to the Sun King's castle, the
Guppies met the Snow Guppy. It was Goby!
When he heard about Gil and Molly's
quest to return the Ring of the Sun, Goby
agreed to help. "You'll need my help going
down the mountain," he said. "Follow me!"

Goby led everyone safely down the mountain. But as they were going over a bridge, the lobster general cast a magic moonbeam, and the bridge began to crumble!

"Bubble Puppy, you've got to get to the Sun King's castle before the sun goes down!" Gil cried.

Bubble Puppy wriggled free and dashed off— just as the rest of the bridge gave way, sending Gil and Molly tumbling!

Gil and Molly fell down, down, down into the realm of the Underguppy. The Underguppy was a mysterious cloaked figure named Nonny. He commanded an army of bats that lived in underground caves.

Nonny showed Gil and Molly the way back to the surface. He also gave them a hoodie of invisibility to help them find Bubble Puppy.

Gil and Molly raced to the Sun King's throne
room. They found Bubble Puppy locked in a cage
and the Night Wizard trying to remove the ring. Gil
used the hoodie of invisibility to free Bubble Puppy
while Molly crept up the throne stairs to awaken
the Sun King.

Gil saw a tapestry that showed the Sun King making the sun rise by pointing the ring at the sun. That gave him an idea.

Gil held Bubble Puppy up to the setting sun. The ring glowed, and the sun began to rise. It was daytime again! The Sun King woke up with a yawn.

"Nooo! My plan is ruined!" cried the
Night Wizard. "Now it will be day again!"

"But daytime is awesome!" said Gil. "You
can play outside with your friends!"

The Night Wizard shook his head. "I don't
have any friends."

Molly smiled. "We'll be your friends!"

And as the warm sun shone down on
everyone, they went outside to play and drink
Bubble Slushies.

"What a wonderful day!" cheered the
Night Wizard, and he smiled at his new
friends. The land of Bubbledom was saved!